THE LUCK THIEVES

CRIME AND MAGIC IN THE NEW RUSSIA #2

JAMES BEACH

MIND
FU

THE LUCK THIEVES

This is a work of fiction. All the characters and events portrayed, except for purposes of satire, are fictional and any resemblance to real people or incidents is purely coincidental.

A Mind Fu original book. 29 Grove St., #340 San Francisco, CA 94102

ISBN: 978-1-945451-07-2

Cover design by James Beach

First printing. June 2018

The doomed man stood the morning gloom of St. Petersburg's snow-covered streets. The man had yet to see Oleg, and thought he was alone. Yet he cast glances nervously around him. Some instinct appeared to be telling the man that all was not well.

Oleg observed the man was in his late sixties, with a hard lined face that had seen many injustices. Perhaps he had been a sailor. Perhaps he'd had enough life experience to know something was wrong without knowing why.

Even though Oleg expected to be invisible to this man, he preferred to take no chances. He approached from behind.

Without warning he thrust his fist into the middle of the man's spine, about parallel with the solar plexus. His victim gasped in sudden pain. Oleg clasped his hand over the old man's mouth, wrapped his other arm around him and dragged him into a nearby alley.

There he shoved the poor bastard to the ground, and checked to make sure they had attracted no suspicion. No one had appeared to notice. Any who might have seen been looking in their direction also should not have seen Oleg, and would think the old man was just another drunk.

Oleg had a job to do, and a life to save. The life to save was his own. The job was ruining the lives of others.

He bent over the man and put his hand on the man's chest. He drew the pattern on him that Magda taught, and began to drain the old man of all the energy he could.

When he had taken most of what he could for the moment, he pulled his hand away to assess what remained of him. The old man's were half-lidded and his face was pale, so much that he was beginning to match the alley's shade of light snow, concrete and filth.

Oleg cursed. The old piece of garbage had barely

enough of what Oleg needed. If his remaining spark could prevail against the cold and grow back into a flame, he could at least provide Oleg with a continuing source, however small. If not, Oleg would have to hunt some more.

So it had been since Oleg was very young. Magda, his owner and tormentor, had come into his life as a child. His first task for her was something he still didn't want to think about - taking similar energy from his fellow orphans, to save his own life.

After so many years, he might be able to be free of her. She would move to a higher level, where he would be out of the range of her concerns. Just a few more lives ruined, and he could at last breathe in relief and start to make a path of his own. Another level of power for Magda meant another level of safety for him.

The man lying at his feet coughed a bit, and opened his eyes. In his last moments he could see Oleg clearly. "You..." the man began. The remaining light in his eyes faded. He breathed his last out into the alley's air.

Oleg stood. He had more work to do before tonight, or Magda would be very angry.

Maybe some day he would be free from her. He didn't dare let himself think of it. For now and the foreseeable future, their destinies were tied. The only path Oleg saw to his own saving was her success.

AURELIAN LEANED BACK in the lumpy couch that was currently his home, and winced. The couch probably dated back to Khrushchev, but the root cause was the bullet hole in Aurelian's back. A painful reminder of his most recent unwanted adventure.

Life as a thief in post-Soviet St. Petersburg had been

hard enough. Then he became ensnared into violent dances with things that should not be.

Still he could not deny his good fortune in being alive. Even more, along the way he had met Lyita. In underground lairs lost since Stalin they had found and destroyed the unholy Ghost Magnet, and saved the entire city.

Then they had returned to the surface, to find the world very much the same. He remained as poor as ever, and still on the run from the law. He had looked high and low for any of the spoils from the Hermitage museum theft that had led to the bullet in his back, to no avail.

At least Lyita had some friends who were not aware of his criminal associations, who gave them a place to stay while he healed. This cramped room and couch weren't much, but they were far warmer than the streets.

After a week Lyita had found new work, and left Aurelian to heal. She had skills as a psychic, a real one - but showing them had always led to her being exploited. So she was looking for a simple way to earn while she figured out her path.

As for himself, he was one of the best working thieves in St. Petersburg. She had not shown much appreciation for this field, and he found himself agreeing with her. But, even though he hated his profession, it still was skills he'd spent effort and risk attaining. Outside of that, he really didn't know that much.

He did know she had been as good and patient with him as any woman could be under the circumstances. Aurelian would have to find work too, and soon. It might even have to be honest.

His Lyita...he did like the sound of that.

She was lovely, and often moody, and smart - maybe smarter than him, although of course it never did a man good to admit something like that. Yet she had stayed with him so far. Maybe she wasn't that smart after all, he laughed to himself.

Not that he was such a bad looking guy. Girls seemed to like him quite a bit. Sure, he was average height. Maybe even a little shorter. But he was also pretty fit from years of getting in and out of buildings, and resourceful enough to have come out alive from many different tight situations.

Whatever her reasons for liking him, he was glad of them. It was time to not make her think too hard about the reasons.

He moved on the couch, wincing more as a result, and snatched the newspaper he had left on the couch's armrest. He looked through the work advertisements again. Maybe there was something he had missed.

Suddenly there was.

Seeking light construction workers. Skilled or unskilled, pay cash at end of day. Meet at the docks at 3pm today.

An address followed, near the Port of St. Petersburg.

The position was perfect for him. How had he missed it?

A chill ran across his back, as if a wind blew across the room. He looked around nervously. The last time he'd felt something similar, he'd ended up shot. This lousy little apartment still shouldn't have a sudden draft like that.

He wished Lyita were here, so at least he could ask her if spirits were involved. Those strange skills of hers helped save them both before.

Aurelian shook his head. Dark magic and a job ad? He did not want to face his woman with fears that sounded like excuses not to work. He locked his foreboding away.

Light construction was something he could do. It might require some sort of kickback to local mafia, but that shouldn't be too bad for a man who knew how to handle himself. There were not usually dangerous people at such a level, just wannabes who dressed up a bit.

That last bit about "3 pm today" was odd. Why not give a specific date? The newspaper was published daily, but still.

Did it matter if this offer was a set up? He liked his girl, and also the streets were cold to sleep on. He had to at least give it a look.

MAGDA LOOKED IN THE MIRROR, as she prepared for the grand event tonight. Her dress was just as she wanted it – neither cheap nor glamorous. She herself appeared exactly as she wanted - neither young or old, neither ugly nor pretty, not tall or short - just another person in the crowd that you would not look twice at. She believed in helping others to underestimate her.

Most of her serfs were working on various tasks related to tonight's aftermath. Only one last thread remained. She picked up her phone and called her assistant. "Did the lure catch today?" asked Magda.

"Yes ma'am!" Oleg answered. The fear in his voice made her smile. It was good to know he would never forget the power she had over him. "I got one, and I felt two more bite. They see a chance, and they both have a lot of luck to lose."

"When might they be done?"

"Mid afternoon."

She closed her eyes and made a fist in triumph. This could seal her ascension. "Do the victims know of magic? We must be especially careful only to hurt peasants, until I become the arbiter."

Oleg paused. She imagined him closing his eyes and feeling the spell. "I don't think they know of any magic," he answered. "They were attuned enough to jump at the lure, but they don't have any magic force themselves."

She frowned. "Two young men is unusual for this spell. Be careful the luck does not shift their way. Where will they be met?"

"They are to be standing outside by the docks this afternoon."

"Good. I am busy with other preparations for tonight. I leave them to you as well."

"As you wish," said Oleg. He decided to brave a joke. "It seems our own luck is doing quite good, eh?"

"It is not due to luck," said Magda. She was all business with no sense of humor. Humor cost time, which was more valuable than money or even luck. "We are where we are because we have made ourselves stronger and wiser than these fools." Her voice hardened. "Don't get distracted. You know what awaits you if you disappoint me."

Her assistant paled, abashed. "Of course, ma'am. I didn't - I didn't mean to-"

"Go do your job." She ended the call, and smiled briefly to herself. They could be disconnected by phone, but he would remain connected to her all his life. As were all who served her – and as soon could be all the new people in her power.

Aurelian decided to not tell Lyita about the possible job. He would either bring her good news, or she would never know it hadn't worked out. He would much rather surprise her pleasantly than disappoint her.

He was just suspicious enough from his thieving career to show up an hour early, and find a spot near a coffee cart to watch who would arrive.

Sure enough, fifteen minutes before the meeting time a man showed up. The man stepped around a corner across the street from where they were supposed to gather, and stood mostly in the shadows. Aurelian's heart sank to watch him, as the man's eyes stayed fixed on the exact corner the ad had asked job-seekers to stand.

The man was thin, a bit on the tall side, with a short bit of blond hair sticking out from a black knit cap. He looked to be in his early thirties, and did not at all look like any kind of an employer. It was not raining or even snowing, yet he was wearing a full-length raincoat more suitable to fancy office workers. He also jumped every time he saw someone walk near the corner, only to relax and then scowl as they walked past it. It all made Aurelian actually curious now. The man was so like a mugger seeking a specific target, except he also seemed completely unfamiliar with this brand of work. His manner was as conspicuous and out of place as his clothes.

After some minutes the guy looked down the street a bit and this time didn't move his head. Aurelian followed his eyes, and saw a young man approaching. The man this apparent amateur mugger was looking at seemed barely old enough to be called a man. He was probably not even 18, a little soft and pudgy too, and with an awful haircut. The kind of kid who does decently at school and goes on to an uneventful life as some sort of plumbing manager or sanitation engineer. Was this kid lured by the promise of construction work too?

The kid stood at the exact spot mentioned in the ad and then looked around, waiting for someone to show up. His back was to the man in the trench coat staring at him.

The likely mugger walked toward the kid.

Aurelian found himself mad enough to take a punch at

this piece of crap. He'd come all the way here for a job, and this kid had too, and it was all just a set up for a mugging? What was the world coming to? Steal from a man if you must – but why set him up with hope and then betray him?

If someone had to steal, they should at least take from people who have things. Not from people who have nothing.

Aurelian left the coffee cart and began walking towards them both, increasing his pace to reach the would-be mugger first. It would simply make his day to ruin the mugging of this poor soft kid. It might take as little as just walking by whistling loud, or asking for a cigarette. Sometimes that's all it took to spoil such a moment.

When he had almost reached the blond man in the full raincoat, the would-be mugger whirled around to face him.

"Got a cigarette?" Aurelian asked, in his best pesky civilian voice.

The man stared at him in surprise. "You can see me?"

Aurelian frowned. "Of course I can see you. Why couldn't I see you? Are you drunk?"

The man muttered beneath his breath and drew a pattern in the air before Aurelian's eyes. The man moved to his left and...

What had Aurelian been thinking? Something about...a kid...

Aurelian felt a sharp pain in his gut, and he sat down hard on the pavement. He looked at his stomach. It felt like something had been ripped out, just below his sternum. But there was no blood. No blood anywhere.

Some sort of blur punched him again, in the same spot. He raised an arm to push him off, and barely saw another strike. Then it was...drawing something on the skin below his sternum where he'd just been hit. But through Aurelian's coat.

Aurelian passed out.

He woke up minutes later and jumped to his feet, to nearly fall again from sudden dizziness. He made it back to his feet by sheer determination, and stared at the streets around him. A couple walked past averting their gaze, probably thinking he was some passed-out drunk. An old man with a cane walked slowly around the corner to a destination unknown. The coffee cart was even gone. There was no one else to fight.

Aurelian patted his pockets. He still had his cellphone, keys and wallet. What was going on?

A groan alerted him to the kid he'd seen before, now on the ground across the street.

He looked up at Aurelian. "Did you do this to me?" he asked, his eyes barely focusing.

"Shut up," said Aurelian, trying to cover his rising panic.

What the hell had just happened?

Magda's cellphone rang. She answered it.

"I got their luck," Oleg confirmed. "You should begin to feel it soon."

"Excellent. That should give more than enough to win tonight, if the others don't first give me what is my right." She paused. It was good to occasionally express gratitude. That also made the fear stick better. "Good work, my assistant."

"Thank you mistress," Oleg said with great relief. "I should tell you there - there was something strange about one of them."

Magda didn't like uncertainty. Even the magic she preferred was direct and brutal. "What?"

"One of them could see me."

She grit her teeth. "Did you just forget to hide your presence?"

"Of course not! Ma'am," he added quickly. "To be extra sure, I nearly doubled the spell."

"And in spending luck energy on that, you drained your own. That is how luck can be," she said. "I've told you this. You do listen to me, don't you?" She increased the anger in her tone, to make sure Oleg could not mistake it for mere annoyance. "When you channel your luck into a spell to take someone else's, you temporarily deplete your own. You will have less luck than you think until you have fully collected all the luck you target. You must be extra careful under these conditions."

"Yes ma'am, I was listening and I know. It's just that the way he looked me in the eyes...I wonder if he's got an immunity to that spell."

She turned her head and considered it. "There was a strange ripple a week ago. Everything felt a little lighter somehow. Perhaps this one you speak of was involved in that, but has not yet been introduced to other circles..." She stared off, remembering her own violent introduction to the world of the impossible and occult, so many years ago. "If he was involved in that, he may have seen some of the beyond. Once even a peasant has seen the impossible, it becomes harder to make them unsee it. And it becomes harder to cloud their sight."

"Okay," said Oleg. "Then what shall we do?"

"As long as he is protected by no patrons, he is free to be hunted." She rubbed her chin. "Drain them both of the rest of their luck as quickly as you can, then finish them off." She looked at her diamond-studded watch. "I must now go to the event. Don't slip up, or I will take all the remaining luck from you. You know that I can."

"Of course, mistress," Oleg said.

She smiled as she ended the call. She liked how he didn't bother to hide his fear from her. She suspected it was because he thought it made him safer from her.

She hailed a taxi for the Hermitage museum. It was too early for the event, but it was always pleasant to look around the museum. Perhaps there were images of Czars or bloody battles she might take inspiration from, as she mentally prepared.

AURELIAN STAGGERED over and helped the kid to his feet. The kid thanked him and mumbled that his name was Eric. They didn't say much else as they helped each other back to their homes.

Eric 's house was first. He told Aurelian his parents weren't home, and invited him in to rest. Aurelian mumbled a thanks and shook his head. He must get back to his own house before he collapsed from whatever had happened to him. What a lucky kid he is to still have living parents, Aurelian thought.

He continued on back to the where he lived from the charity of Lyita's friends. He barely made it up the steps and fumbled with the keys, nearly dropping them three times in a row. He could have picked the lock if he needed to, but it was still disheartening. It was as if he was straining against some force to just do ordinary things. Like a rubber band, or maybe a leech, was pulling something out of him that he needed for every step.

He made it up the stairs while nearly slipping and falling three times. At last he reached the room where he'd been staying, made it to the couch, and then collapsed.

Hours later, Lyita knocked at the door. She had her hands full with groceries, and couldn't quite get to the knob. Aurelian had to hear her - why didn't he answer?

She managed to get the door open, and came in still struggling with packages. There he was on the couch, lying almost exactly where he'd been when she'd left for work in the morning.

Her face fell. He had been well earlier today. Was he taking a turn for the worse?

A separate thought occurred to her, that made her feel ashamed. He had shown such bravery a few days ago. Together they had saved each other's lives. Yet they still knew so little about each other. What if he turned out to be an addict of some kind? Or just a drunk?

Or neither, but just another lazy child who thought he was a man.

She knew he was still recovering. But hunger and the embarrassment of relying on charity, sometimes outweighed the need of the body to heal up in a comfortable fashion. This wasn't some fat nation where they could take their time figuring out how to survive. She was working at a coffee shop in the airport, where foreign tourists leered at her. They would leave single Ruble tips like they were high rollers. Especially when she was tired, it took such work to shut away their thoughts. But she did what she had to do. If she had to work, he had better find work too.

She put the packages down on the floor. One of the bags ripped open, and a can rolled out. It rolled straight over to the couch near Aurelian's foot, as if it were drawn there.

She shut the door. He did not move. She coughed, and still he didn't stir. "Aurelian!" she said at last. "Wake up!"

Aurelian did so, and got to this feet in a rush - stepping on the can. It rolled to the side and he pitched in the opposite direction. She rushed over and managed to help catch him - he had very nearly brained himself on the couch's cheap, sharp-cornered wooden armrest.

"What is up with you?" she asked. "I have never seen you so clumsy - are you drunk?"

"I wish. Then I could forget the last few hours." He doubled over, his stomach hurting. There was a soft thud behind them. They turned to see her shopping bag had fallen over, and several more cans rolled over from the bag to beneath his feet.

"What happened?" she asked.

"I saw a job in the paper, light construction. I went to check it out and..." He paused. "This will sound crazy. But a man did something to me, I don't know what. And ever since then," he looked at the cans gathered beneath his feet, "It's like random things are trying to kill me."

She became annoyed. "Don't be ridic-" she began, and heard a ripping noise from above her head. They looked up to see a section of the cheap plaster ceiling began to separate. He tried to move out of its way but couldn't find his feet. She pulled him a little further out of the way, and a section of ceiling landed just missed him to bounce off of the couch.

Aurelian clenched his fists and stared upwards at the ceiling. "What is happening? Are there ghosts around?"

Her eyes widened. "I don't think so." She closed her eyes for a second, and then shook her head. "Lost souls are not behind this."

He shook his head. "I've never had this much bad luck in my life!"

"How is your wound?"

"Alright, I guess. It is starting to hurt some more..."

"We are going to have to go back there someday soon,

you know," she said. "To the Ghost Magnet. We can't leave it like that. Someone else might come across it and start the whole thing up again."

"I know I know," he coughed. "This doesn't seem like the right time for that just yet."

"So tell me what happened."

He didn't want to admit misfortune, let alone have her see him as weak. But what else could he say? "I answered an ad for work down by the docks," he sighed. "There was another kid who I think came from the same ad and - someone else. I barely saw him. He - it was like he reached his hand in here," he pointed to his sternum, "and took something from me *through my skin*."

She pulled up his shirt and felt his stomach, finding no wound or even a cut. She felt his forehead. He pushed her hand away. "I don't have a fever! This happened."

"Alright," she said.

The little touch of doubt she showed hurt harder than any other pain. "Wouldn't I invent a better lie? Since then nothing has been the same. You see all the things going wrong for me. Everything!"

"Maybe it's just...maybe something about today."

A knock came from the door. Lyita left the couch and opened it, to see one of their hosts.

The man was not happy. "Lyita, what is going on here? I hear things rolling and crashing all over the place. We're trying to put our kids to bed."

"I don't know," said Lyita. "Aurelian is having a bad day."

"Not here he isn't. Not any more. You, you can stay." He looked over her shoulder, saw Aurelian on the couch and scowled. "You, get your things and go. We've had enough."

"Come on," said Aurelian. "I just started looking for work. It's only been a week!"

"A week too long. Get moving. If you're not gone in an hour I'm calling the police." He nodded in satisfaction, and went back downstairs.

She closed the door, came back to the couch and sat next to him. "Okay," she admitted. "That's all a little weird."

"All I did was go out for a job I saw in the paper, and - I saw someone for a few seconds. He looked like he was about to mug someone, and I didn't like it. So I approached him. Then I was hurt. Right here." He pointed at just beneath his sternum. "Like he stabbed me and took something out."

"Where is the ad?"

"Right here." He reached over for the newspaper, still on the armrest where he'd left it. He flipped to the classified section.

The advertisement was gone.

Aurelian leaned back and put his hand over his eyes. "It's like I'm..." he stopped rather than complete the sentence. It was hard enough to admit he'd had trouble. He didn't want Lyita to lose more faith in him, by suggesting he could be losing his mind.

"Ever see anything like that?" he pointed at the ceiling.

A broom knocked into the floor beneath them. "58 minutes!" came the voice from below.

"This isn't normal," said Aurelian. "It's not anywhere near normal." He unsteadily got to his feet.

"Where are you going to go?"

"Some university kid got hit by the same thing that hit me. Maybe he knows something. Maybe he's a part of it." Aurelian picked up his coat and managed to put it back on.

"I'm coming with you."

"Like hell you are. I don't want you getting involved." His face softened. "I don't want you to get pulled into – whatever is happening to me."

"Whatever is happening, it's affecting me now anyway," Lyita pointed out. She yelled down to the floor. "We're going out! And screw yourselves!"

He gripped the rail tightly as they walked down the stairs. They exited onto the street.

"I don't want to jinx you too. I really wish you'd stay back." He tried to cajole her. "It's warm back there too."

"Yes, it is," she agreed. "Also you are wounded and I am with you."

"I love you for this." They both paused for a second, for the step he just had taken. This was the first time either of them had mentioned love.

"Steal me flowers later then," she told him with a smile.

THEY WALKED BACK to where he had parted ways with that Eric kid. It was a three story apartment building, sort of a Victorian row house as it was called. It had started as a tenement for ship builders and their families, then probably housing for mid-level Communist party members. Now it was on its way to becoming classic because it had been too worthless to replace in the intervening years.

Aurelian knocked on the door. A splinter stuck in his hand. "Seriously?" he said out loud as he pulled it out. He wrapped his jacket sleeve around his hand and pounded on the door. "Open up you punk! If you know what's good for you!"

There was no answer. He considered the building type. There should be two apartments per floor and a winding interior staircase between them. Even in a city like St. Petersburg, sometimes people left their second story windows unlocked.

If he could get in through the first apartment to his right, he could reach the stairwell. His left shoulder would hurt, but he should be able to favor his right shoulder enough to handle a single story.

He started to climb over the front steps' railing, to reach the lower story window ledge.

"What are you doing?" hissed Lyita.

"Shh! I told you. I might have to break in."

"Come down from there before..."

Just as she started speaking, a police car started down the street. He hopped off the other side of the railing and hid behind some trash barrels. Lyita took out a cigarette, to pretend she was outside to have a smoke.

The police car shined a light on her briefly, then passed around the corner.

"Are you okay?" she asked him.

"Almost twisted my ankle," he sighed. He walked back to the steps.

"You really can't take risks like that right now," said Lyita. "You know the police are still looking for you."

"Then what should I do?" asked Aurelian.

"I don't know!" said Lyita. "But you have to be careful."

Aurelian had a thought, that he couldn't really explain with words. "Could you try knocking on the door?"

Lyita looked at him curiously, but did so. They were rewarded with a muffled groan that came through the door. "Who is it?" asked a younger male voice. "Go 'way, I'm trying to sleep."

"That's him," said Aurelian. "Come to the door Eric! We have to talk. I know what's happened to you, it's the same thing that happened to me."

There was a short silence, and then the sounds of doors unlocking and footsteps in the hallway. The outer door opened, and the kid appeared. His face looked haunted.

"What happened to us?" the kid asked.

"I don't really know," Aurelian confessed. "I'm hoping we can find out."

Eric sighed and let them in.

As Magda luxuriated in the luck energy channeling into her, she admired a painting of the torture of a saint. She felt many missed the true lesson of such a saint's example. A man who would sacrifice himself for others deserved torture, for being such a fool.

The power from the weak would always accrue to people like her. Through tools of magic like the tattoo like her mother gave her, and her mother before. Surviving when others died, and now taking power from others so they would either die or serve her.

As Magda turned to see another painting, she felt a sudden lessening of luck.

She called up Oleg. "What is happening? Where is the luck going?"

"I just felt it change too. I don't know! It's like both of their luck is changing."

She snarled. "Handle it. These two had better keep giving us what we need. Or your luck will definitely change."

"Yes ma'am."

She hung up the cellphone.

"Nice apartment," said Aurelian.

"Thanks," Eric said woodenly. "Really, it's my parent's apartment, while I go to engineering school."

"Fascinating," said Lyita. "Now what in hell is going on?"

"I don't know," said Eric miserably. "I feel like crap and it's like I can't do anything right. Do you mind if I sit?" He led them to the living room, and fell on his own couch. They each took a nearby chair. Aurelian sat in his with great care, making sure to not go near the coffee table which currently held a laptop. He looked up at the ceiling. It didn't seem to show any cracks.

He looked over at Eric, and noted the kid still wasn't too weary to be sneaking eyefuls of Lyita. He didn't really blame him. A beautiful woman can have that effect on anyone.

"Same here," Aurelian agreed. "It's like everything is going wrong. It's like I'm trying just as hard or even harder, and every possible thing is going against me. It's like a damn gypsy curse."

Lyita shook her head, and then looked thoughtful. "Those aren't real. But that does remind me..."

"What?"

"You know my parents pretended to be gypsy fortunetellers, before..." Aurelian saw her stop. She never talked of how her parents had died. "Sometimes they would come along someone who had a black cloud over their fortune."

"But I thought that your parents' fortunetelling was a con."

"It was! And yet they still couldn't even get a good reading. The cards would be impossibly against them. My mother would try her best to cheat with the cards to get a happy reading for a tip, and the cards wouldn't even allow it."

Aurelian frowned. "Was this in St. Petersburg?"

"At the edge."

"That's impossible," Eric insisted. Aurelian saw that he

was offended by the very idea. "I'm an engineering student. I know these things."

Aurelian shook his head. "I've seen some things that are supposed to be impossible."

Eric sputtered, "No! Tarot readings aren't real. They're just probability and random chance, and people wanting to see what they want to see."

"Most of the time," said Lyita. "But not these times. I've seen it myself."

"But there's no such thing as – as things that can't be explained!" Eric persisted.

Aurelian threw up his hands, and nearly knocked over the lamp next to him on the table. It was only barely caught by Lyita.

Aurelian snapped his fingers. "I've got an idea. Eric, do you have any change?"

The kid frowned, and dug a 5-ruble coin out of his pocket. "Like this?"

"Sure. It's normal, right?"

Eric turned it over in his hands carefully, and hefted it in his hand. "Yes. Why?"

"Pick the number or statue." The number was generally considered the front side of the coin, and the statue was the back.

"Statue," said Eric.

"Now flip it. Carefully, so it doesn't knock one of our eyes out."

Eric flipped the coin into the air and trapped it on the back of his hand.

The number side was up. "That's just 50% every time," the kid protested.

"Actually no," said Aurelian. "I read about it. In normal circumstances, for reasons no one understands, it's slightly more often the same side that was facing up when it was flipped. 51 out of 100 or something."

"Where did you hear that?" asked Lyita.

"Some American adventure novel. Anyways, call it again."

"Fine. The statue." Eric flipped it. It landed with the number facing up. "The number then," he said, and flipped it. This time it was the statue.

The kid stared at the coin in his own hand for a second, as if it had betrayed him. "It's just not possible to control probability like that!" he protested.

"I have stayed alive by recognizing reality the way it is," Aurelian asserted. "Reality doesn't care if we understand it. It happens regardless." He pointed at the coin in Eric's hand. "You try it as long as you like. Just call it before you flip it."

The kid kept trying. After 20 tries he stopped. It had not come out as he called it once. "So, what are you saying that means?" he asked.

"Someone took something from us, and without it what we want turns against us. Whatever it is, we might even need it just to live. I'm feeling worse and worse, and so are you."

"So, what can we do?" Eric asked, sitting back in his chair and looking at him for guidance, as if he was now Eric's trusted older brother.

"I don't know," Aurelian confessed.

Magda felt the situation change further. She cursed. The event would start in a matter of hours, the culmination of years of work. Yet she had to put all that aside to fix a mess that shouldn't even be an issue.

She dialed Oleg, her fingers stabbing at the phone in anger.

Oleg answered before she could speak. "I don't know what's going on, I can feel it too!"

She put her hand to her forehead. "They must be starting to understand their luck, you idiot!" said Magda. "That gives them a chance to change their fortune!"

"I'm trying to find them. It's getting harder to follow the drain."

She grit her teeth, and closed her eyes. With her own greater experience in this magic, she should be able to narrow it down. "They are due north of you, about 500 meters. Once you get within 100, you should be able to feel them and get it done." She opened her eyes. "Now get moving and get it done. If you handle it in time you can share in my success. If you don't, you'd better start running." She clicked off.

That should do it. He just needed the proper motivation.

She sat on a bench set in front of another priceless painting, and closed her eyes to visualized her moment of triumph. She would ascend the marble steps to the room in the museum known only to a few. Around her, other people of knowledge and power also gathered, and took their places along the patterns carved into the marble floor. All would be dressed in fine clothes that befit the occasion and as was tradition.

She would walk in, a smooth tower of confident power, and the rest of the room would pause and come to silence from sheer awe. They would drift out of her way like prey avoiding the path of a lioness.

She take her place, and the ritual would start. The sky and stars would align with the time and place of the desires of all gathered. Then Roths, that most recent sanctimonious bastard who had stood in her way for several years now, would know he was spending his last few minutes drawing breath. He would have no choice but to swallow with trepidation and begin.

The ceiling would open, and the milk light of the moon would drift forth and settle on her. She would take Roths place as the new arbitrator, for all the hidden powers of St. Petersburg. A head to manage their occult affairs. A power she could use to bring all into her sway, and bring the old rules down.

Spells cast ages ago would become undone, and she would recast their games of spirit and even death to her great benefit. All because she had striven to learn what so few understood. They had no idea how much the selection process of an arbiter was based on...simple luck.

"It feels like I'm - I feel better suddenly," said Eric.

"Me too!" Aurelian realized.

"Just like that?" Lyita frowned. "It seems too easy."

Aurelian laughed suddenly. "I would get a drink, but the bottle could still crack in my hand."

Eric shrugged. "We have no liquor anyway. My parents don't drink."

Aurelian raised his eyebrows. "What? Where are they from?"

"My mom is from the Netherlands." Eric sighed. "She's a religious separatist, she moved here during Glasnost. We can't even have beer in the house. So lame."

Lyita placed her hand on Aurelian's arm. "We still don't know what happened. Why is it suddenly better?"

Aurelian frowned. "You're right. We need to-" he heard a

creak from the floorboards outside the door. "Sh!" he whispered. "Did you hear that?"

"No," said Eric and Lyita at the same time.

Aurelian put his fingers to his lips. They fell silent as he wondered, why would someone be trying to hide their entrance?

There could only be one reason. Aurelian gathered them in close, speaking very softly. "That can only be someone involved in this. Eric, if someone knocks, open the door and step back inside. If it looks like the man who stole our luck, just let him in."

Lyita shook her head. "Aurelian, that won't-"

"Sh!" said Aurelian. "This might be one shot." His eyes ran over the living room, looking for anything he could use. He grabbed a nearby table lamp and unplugged it from the wall. It was now a mediocre club.

"But-" Lyita persisted.

There was a knock at the door. Aurelian stood to one side, where he would be hidden by the opening door. Lyita was fuming to speak.

Eric looked at Aurelian and then Lyita with uncertainty.

The knock came again. "Who is it?" asked the kid.

"Good news," said the same voice Aurelian had heard before. "If you can let me in, I have an offer. Your fortunes are about to change." Aurelian heard a chuckle in the tone, as if this was a private joke no one else would get. He tightened his grip on the lamp.

Eric opened the door. Through the crack Aurelian could saw it was the same man from the docks earlier today.

The man smiled at Eric. "Is your friend here too?"

"I'm, I'm, it's just-"

The luck thief sprang in, lunging straight at the kid.

Aurelian saw he had a knife, and was going straight for the spot right below the sternum.

Aurelian swung the lamp at the bastard's head - and his foot became tangled in a throw rug. The lamp glanced off of the luck thief's shoulder as Aurelian fell to one knee, dropping the lamp.

The man stepped out of his way, snarling. "You're done, fool! Just relax and let death come quickly."

Lyita sprang forward, wrapping her arms around the man. He struggled to free himself. Eric stepped in to help and nearly stumbled onto the attacker's knife. Lyita barely twisted the assailant to the side before he shoved her away. She slammed against the wall.

Enraged, Aurelian got to his feet and kicked at the man. This time he connected with the luck thief's midsection. The man growled and wildly swung his knife in a long arc. Aurelian leapt back of out of the way, slipped on the rug again and fell backwards to the ground. The man looked at both him and the kid on the ground, not knowing who to attack first.

Lyita picked up a chair and threw it at their attacker. It thudded into the side of his head. "Ow, bitch!" he said. "After these two you're next!"

Aurelian decided not to get up from the ground. His luck wasn't that good standing. He pushed forward with his hands and kicked at the luck thief's leg and hit his ankle. The thief went down to one knee.

Lyita picked up the lamp Aurelian had dropped and smashed it against the side of the luck thief's. He staggered and fell back against the wall. He pushed his knife you to hold them back, and touched his head. Blood was on his fingers. "This shouldn't be possible. Our destiny arrives tonight!"

Eric stumbled to his feet, and with a wild yell charged right at the luck thief. "No!" Aurelian exclaimed "Stay back! Keep your dist-"

With a soft and obscene thunk, the man's knife sank into Eric's stomach up to the hilt.

"But..." said Eric, looking down at the blade protruding from his body.

Aurelian and Lyita watched in shock as what looked like white glowing mist emerge from Eric's torso, so mingle with blood upon the blade.

Eric fell off the knife and thudded to the floor.

The thief raised his arms in triumph. "Yes! That's it! And now..."

Aurelian took a chance on his own bad luck. He got to his feet, and kicked sideways at the thief's arm. The knife flew loose, breaking a bone in the thief's forearm.

Fear sparked in the luck thief's eyes. "You're going to lose!I've got enough luck now to do you too!"

"Try it," snarled Aurelian as he got to this feet and rushed the luck thief. They swung fists at each other. Aurelian kept missing, while the luck thief connected with every punch. Aurelian was dazed, but grappled him into a bear hug just long enough for Lyita to pick up the lamp again. Lyita swung it down with all her might, hitting the luck thief again but also hitting Aurelian.

Aurelian fell to one knee, somewhat dazed. Thinking about what might happen to Lyita if he failed, he forced his unconsciousness away and lunged with both hands for the luck thief's throat. His hands missed and hit the man in the chest, still surprising the man enough to fall backward into the door.

Aurelian put all of his will into one remaining swing at

the side of the luck thief's head. Somehow this one connected.

The luck thief held still just long enough for Lyita to slam the lamp into his head. He slumped against the door and slid to the ground, unconscious.

They rushed over to Eric. Aurelian tried to find his pulse.

"He is already dead," said Lyita.

"That poor…" His eyes teared up and he looked away. "How is any of this possible?" he said at last.

Aurelian felt his own sternum, and then looked at the unconscious luck thief. Following a hunch, he kneeled down next to him and pulled up jacket and shirt.

A complex tattoo of interlocking spheres and abstract symbols covered the luck thief's sternum, the design emanating outwards to fade into his skin. In a certain angle of the room's dim lighting, Aurelian could swear he saw thin and misty tendrils leading from this man's sternum to his own.

"Baby," Lyita said softly. "Maybe we should go, right now. With the way your luck is going, maybe more of his type will come soon."

"That's what I have to fix," said Aurelian. "My luck."

He didn't see any other way forward, than what he was about to do.

He reached into his coat and put on his winter gloves. Then he checked the luck thief's body, taking a cellphone, a wallet, some keys and what looked like an invite to a formal dress affair.

He went to the kitchen and brought back a steak knife. He looked at Lyita. "Now I…have to do something that you might not want to see."

Her mouth was tight, but she nodded. "I trust you."

He hesitated a moment, and then plunged the knife into Eric's dead body. Lyita held her hand to her mouth in surprise. Aurelian then wiped off the handle, and placed it in the luck thief's hand.

He then picked up the luck thief's knife, and kneeled next to him.

Aurelian found himself thinking back to when he was just a child, on his father's farm. His father had slaughtered a pig in front of him to, as he said, "toughen the punk kid up." The pig was tied down. It could tell somehow what was coming, and was squealing.

When Aurelian had tried to look away, his father had cursed and grabbed his chin, pulling his head back towards the sight. "A man looks!" his father said, feeling some kind of glory in the moment. "See where your food comes from!"

Aurelian had waited until his father was just about to strike and closed his eyes. He had done this half from not wanting to see, and half from wanting to defy his father.

He looked down at the luck thief now, and Eric's body laying next to him. He cursed his own squeamishness. and slashed the knife across the exposed side of the man's throat. The luck thief's blood washed across the floor.

Part of what had been taken from Aurelian began to return. He tried not to think of how killing this man had made that occur.

Then Aurelian nearly slipped and nearly stepped in the growing pool of blood, mingled with both the luck thief and his victim. He composed himself, and placed the luck thief's knife in Eric's hand.

He and Lyita wiped clean everything in the room they'd touched, and they left the apartment door open on their way out. Lyita wanted to leave the apartment building through the front, but Aurelian insisted they go up the stairwell to the rooftop and find another way out. As they got to the roof, they could hear sirens approaching. They carefully crossed two rooftops to the west, and went down that building's fire escape to an alley.

For now, Aurelian's luck held. He felt better, that way at least. He didn't know how to feel about what he'd just done.

This was the first time in his life that he'd had to kill a man. How would it affect him? He did not know. Perhaps he still was numb.

As they walked back to where Lyita's friends were no longer allowing Aurelian was to stay, Aurelian felt the ring of the dead luck thief's cellphone. He looked at it for a second, motioned Lyita to silence, and took the call.

"Oleg?" said a voice. It sounded like a woman of late middle age. After a couple of moments with no answer, she said "It seems my assistant has run out of luck."

Aurelian snorted a dark laugh but said no more.

The woman sighed. "He was with me a long time, and very useful to me. So my message to you is: you take care of yourself. Make sure you live long enough for me to end you."

Aurelian looked at the phone, and memorized her number. He took out the phone's battery and network card, smashed them both, and dropped them in the sewer. His blood-covered winter gloves quickly followed.

"Now what?" Lyita asked quietly.

"I have no idea," Aurelian admitted. He breathed out. "But I'm pretty sure we shouldn't wait for her. It seems like that's how whatever luck we have will run out." He thought of Eric again, and his jaw tightened. "That poor stupid kid. His parents will find him."

Lyita nodded sadly. "Someone should pay." She

embraced him. "Just like that piece of crap who tried to kill my man."

He held her close and kissed her hair. "You are fantastic."

She let go and punched him lightly in his chest. "You'd be wise to remember that."

Aurelian pulled out the dead luck thief's wallet, and looked through it. There was no identification, little money, and a ticket to an event.

"Something tonight?" she read over his shoulder. "At the Hermitage museum?"

He nodded. "He said something about his destiny arriving tonight? Him and someone else?" He clenched his teeth. "I am so sick of this not knowing what is going on!"

"I know baby. But whatever it is, I don't think we can hide from it."

He nodded. "Going forward is the best bet."

"Do you think we can get in?"

Aurelian smiled. "Did you forget you were associating with a thief? I was in the Hermitage just over a week ago." His face grew serious. "But 'we' aren't getting in. You're going back to your friends' place. This is too dangerous."

She frowned and shook her head. "You're smarter than that. You barely have the luck to not fall down, even now. Don't make me hurt you."

"I have the ticket," said Aurelian. "Only one of us can get in."

"Is that so?" she said, folding her arms. "And you are sure it will be you? With the way your luck has been going?"

"Of course," he lied.

She was not fooled. "Just accept it. I'm going with you."

She would not budge.

They stopped back at her friends' place. From the

sounds in their apartment, they were apparently having dinner. They had helpfully piled Aurelian's few belongings in the downstairs hallway.

Aurelian sighed, dug through them and selected his most presentable outfit. It was a nicer set of boots, cleaner blue jeans and a sweater.

Lyita went upstairs, and returned in a dress that made her look both stunning and more herself than ever. Aurelian shook his head. It was girl magic, forbidden to men.

They spent entirely too much money on a cab straight to the Hermitage. Aurelian asked the driver to go the long way around it, along the Palace Square. Most of the length of the museum could be seen this way. It was lit by the moon and very beautiful.

The main entrance itself was smaller than one might expect for one of the largest museums in the world. This was because the building itself had originally been made for the convenience of royalty of course, and not for access to the general public. Let alone access for thieves.

As the cab drove around the outside of the Palace Square, they saw some lights were on inside the museum. This must be the private event that was indicated by the strange text on the ticket. Large men in plain clothes had even been placed outside, along the ramp right before the entrance.

They reached the end of the palace square. Aurelian instructed the driver to pull over at the next corner. They exited the cab, and Aurelian tipped the driver well. After all, either this would work or he would have no more need for money.

The taxi drove off, leaving them alone on the street. "I've never broken into a building before," Lyita confessed. "How should we do this?"

Aurelian took Lyita's hands in his. "You just go in with that ticket, and act like you know exactly what you're doing there. When you're inside, find your way to the main stairway to the second floor, and then walk down the hall all the way to the east side of the building. You'll find a ladies' room. Open that window and text me when it's done." He pointed at a window about thirty feet high, just beneath a bridge-like structure that connected two different wings of the museum. "Or text me if you can't."

She looked at the window. "You can get all the way up there?"

"It's how I got in the last time."

"I don't like this plan at all. Can you still climb?" She let go of his hand to feel his back.

He tried not to wince from the pressure near his wound, took back her hand in his and squeezed. "Of course I can." He didn't add, because he had to.

"If you're sure then," she said.

"Trust me."

"I do," she said, and kissed him. She let go of his hands and let her hand trail on his chest, her eyes telling him to be careful. Then she walked back towards the front museum steps.

He stepped away and around the corner, peeking his head around to watch. She walked up to the first guard and presented her ticket. He examined it, and then her, and for a frightening second he thought Lyita might be in real trouble. Then the guard handed the invitation back to her, and nodded to his companions.

Aurelian immediately walked around the side of the building to directly below the window. As soon as he heard the window open, all he would have to do is hop the iron fence behind him. The bridge structure would hide his climbing from the street.

He performed some warmup exercises, and waited. He wished he'd had the time to get new gloves. The wall would be cold, and the night was only getting colder.

He waited a bit longer.

And then...

He barely moved his head out of the way as something flew past, to smack into the wall. On instinct he dove and rolled, coming to his feet to the side of his assailant.

A middle-aged woman dressed in a fine fur overcoat, against the cold of the evening. Eyes glared at him from an otherwise mundane face, such as one would pass on the street without a second thought.

How had she gotten so close without him even hearing her?

He leaned to the side to look around her. Was the man who struck at him behind her? Had she thrown a rock?

Then he saw the designs glowing in the air around her clenched fists. The patterns themselves reminded him of the tattoos on the body of the man he'd killed earlier today.

"You must be the bitch on the phone," said Aurelian.

"You must be about to die!" She ran at him swinging.

He'd never been a purist for fighting fairly, even if his opponent wasn't wielding glowing fists. He kicked at her stomach.

She blocked most of it with her fist. He screamed in pain from where she touched him. It was as if he'd been hit by lightning in his shin. His kick was deflected further by her winter coat, and only knocked her back slightly.

He tried to kick with his other leg, and nearly fell. Suddenly he realized the leg he'd hit her with felt weaker.

"You feel the drain?" she sneered. "This is what you are

messing with. This is what you brought on yourself when you killed my servant."

"He tried to kill us, you crazy bitch!"

"The rat has no say in the actions of a cat." She moved in closer, cutting off escape back to the street. "Let alone how much the rat is hurt."

"I am thief, and a damn good one," he stated with pride. "But I would never take someone's luck."

"That is why you will-"

He ran to her left before she finished her response. She moved in and blocked that way, cutting the distance between them. She began backing up to the iron fence behind him. He faked to the left, and then faked to the right to run left again for real.

Her glowing fist caught him straight just where his stomach met his sternum, where his luck had been taken from before. He doubled over and collapsed to the ground, choking and vomiting.

She stood over him, relishing the moment. "This is what you get, when you face someone in full command of magic." She began pummeling from above, pounding his head and back. Each blow a searing pain. He tried to crawl forward. She leaned over, to strike him some more.

He rolled out of her way, and kicked back at her, pushing her off balance. She fell backwards and lost her feet. He got up, and briefly thought of running to the street.

She got up before he could, and beckoned him towards her with a sneer. He shook his head and looked around for something to swing with. A broken bottle, anything. And as his current luck would have it, this alley next to the Hermitage museum was one of the cleanest alleys he'd ever seen.

She cornered him again and began to strike. He dodged

as well he could, and swung back as fast and hard as he could find. Every time her hand even touched him it stung and his whole body convulsed with pain. He fell, and began to lose consciousness as the blows rained down. He reached forward to pull himself away, as he racked his stunned mind for some way out of this, some chance to make his way clear, just live a moment longer.

"Yes, this way!" he cried. "Police! She's a murderer!"

She turned to see where he was looking. With the last remaining energy he could muster he rushed to the corner of the alley and began to climb.

She realized his plan, and screeched in rage as she ran at him. He pulled the ankle of his still-stinging leg just out of her reach.

Ten feet, he told himself. If he could get just ten feet up. Just the rim of lower retaining wall, then hand on that drain pipe, just enough to swing over to the bottom of the Hermitage's thankfully ornate window ledge with enough room to plant both feet, and then...

He made it.

His back to her, gripping the top of the window's edge a scant few feet above her, he looked down over his shoulder and into her blazing eyes.

"Coward!" she demanded. "Come down here and face your fate!"

"Thanks so much for the kind offer, but I'm good here."

She screeched and tried to climb after him, but could only get a grip on the top of the lower retaining wall before she slipped back to the ground. "You can't stay there all night!"

He spat some blood. "Neither can you, I think."

"What kind of a man runs from a fight?"

Woozy from his beating, he laughed. He lost his grip and

dropped back to the lower ledge. He jumped back up just in time, and scrambled to keep his legs out of her reach again.

He laughed again, his knuckles whitening with his grip on the wall. "A survivor."

A beeping noise echoed lightly off the walls. Unsure what to do, she stepped back.

"Please, don't be late for your appointment on my account."

She sneered. "This is not over! There won't be a wall big enough for you to climb once this night is done!"

She adjusted her dress with a huff, and stormed off.

In his stunned daze, he realized that she actually felt he had wronged her. He shook his head. What was wrong with people?

He focused back on this moment. What to do now?

There was only one answer. He sighed.

He leaned over to the drain pipe. Since he was on the side that was exposed to the street, he climbed up the pipe as quickly as he could. When he reached the third floor landing, he walked above the connecting bridge.

It appeared he had not been seen yet. So good so far.

His heart was also beating much faster than it should have been, and his upper back was moving on from discomfort and into searing pain. It would have been easer if he weren't still recovering with his wound, let alone taken a beating. How much he could trust that bribed veterinarian's stitches to hold his wound together?

Gritting his teeth, he edged along the ledge until he reached the window.

LYITA FOLLOWED other persons through the building's main

entrance. She examined everything around her as closely as she could while still looking like she knew exactly where she was going. It was easy to seem cool on the outside, but this place made her deeply nervous. This was high society, and nothing she'd ever been a part of in her life. She knew how to look good in a dress. But who knew what sort of elite social cue she could miss, that would reveal her poor origins?

She found the stairwell that Aurelian said would lead to the bathroom with the window. She was about to head up. A large man in an impeccable suit stepped before her, with the unmistakable manner of a sentry.

"My apologies, but you cannot enter the other parts of the museum."

"Oh," said Lyita. She put on her best little girl impression. Most macho guys fell for it immediately. "But I just want to powder my nose."

The guard smiled apologetically. "If it were up to me, you could do that and then come to the gathering. But the Arbiter does not want others sniffing around his sanctuary. You understand."

Lyita froze her face to hide her confusion. "Yes, of course. Silly of me." She walked towards the same area all of the other entrants were congregating in. As she did, she pulled out her cellphone to warn Aurelian she couldn't reach the window.

As she took a step past the threshold, her cellphone screen went blank as if it was turned off. She tapped the screen a few more times, then tried to reboot it. It was simply not working at all.

Her anxiety increased to feverish levels. How was she going to get Aurelian in here? Was she going to have to manage this all on her own?

She spun around to go back outside, just as the door was closed behind her. She swallowed and faced the room.

There were about 30 other people in there with her, about evenly males and females. All were well dressed, but some seemed quite out of place. She noticed strange tattoos on some of the men and women, occasionally extending to their faces. Her parents attempts to profit from her psychic abilities in various schemes had led to occasional associations with criminal circles; as a result, she had grown up familiar with prison tattoos. She was also familiar with some of the more stylish tattoos that were popular with club goers for years now. These tattoos were unlike any she had seen before. The patterns were complex, and hard to comprehend. Some of them were hard to even see, and appeared to emerge only if their owners' skin was in shadow. None of the tattoos looked exactly like what they had seen on the luck thief's body. None looked entirely different either.

Other denizens of the space might have looked completely comfortable behind a lunch counter. One man was even wearing the uniform of a city bus driver, and had brought a cat. The man stared ahead bored, as the cat eyed her with curiosity.

The room itself had three entrances, evenly spaced around its edge. There was just enough floor area for the amount of people gathered to be comfortable. It was a half dome, rising from the floor to about 50 feet in height. The walls were solid black marble all the way around and to a height of roughly ten meters, where the wall blended seamlessly into a curving sheet of glass. This glass continued the shape of the hemisphere all the way to a center at the top. There, in the last few feet before the dome's apex was a circular metal grid in a peculiar pattern.

The space was striking. Why had she never heard of such a room in the Hermitage before?

The moon shone bright tonight, and was just beginning to rise over the bottom wall of the hemisphere. A few more people trailed into the room from other doors. The people began organizing themselves according to the lines upon the floor. She then noticed the lines set into the marble floor that matched the pattern in the highest part of the domed ceiling.

She found what appeared to be an open spot in that same pattern and stood there, determined to bluff her way through as long as she could.

Across the room, a woman in a fine fur overcoat stared at her. She appeared neither young nor old, neither fat nor thin, neither lovely nor plain.

She smiled at Lyita, in way that was utterly carnivorous.

AURELIAN STARED in frustration as the window stayed closed. He checked his cellphone for the third time, and still Lyita had sent him no response. It was cold and getting colder. The physical exertion kept him warm inside, but his exposed fingers were starting to get stiff.

He cursed. Breaking the window was a risk. The only other way to get in without detection was, in his current state, almost unthinkable. He'd have to clamber onto the slanted copper roof, slick with light snow, and try the maintenance entrance. And hope that he still remembered the codes to the door, and that they hadn't been changed since the failed theft he'd been a part of just over a week ago.

At that exact moment, a piece of the ledge he stood on crumbled under his feet. He twisted for a grip as he fell, and barely caught himself on the now broken edge. His shoulder hurt so hard he actually let out a noise.

Keeping his mind focused to try and overwhelm any possibility of luck being needed, he pulled himself back up, thinking through every finger and toe hold on the wall. Inch by inch, he hauled himself back over the ledge. There were a couple of further crumblings of brick which could have killed him if he were paying any less than absolute attention. He lay flat on the edge, to reduce the amount of his weight per square centimeter, and stopped for breath.

What was he going to do?

He had no tools and still had bad luck. While Lyita was still inside there, stuck with whatever magical nutcases he had pulled her into. While she was trying to help save him.

Magda's taunts still stung. He was damned if was going to let Lyita die trying to save him from a woman he had run from.

He inched ahead on the ledge, to see where the ledge had crumbled and parted from the wall. That had actually been weird. Taking utmost care, he leaned over the place where the ledge was missing to see what else might be gone.

Sure enough, some parts of the exterior wall itself had fallen with the ledge. What could have killed him might also be his opportunity.

Very carefully he reached over the edge, and removed further crumbling pieces from the wall. He placed them on the ledge behind him rather than letting them drop and make a single sound. Soon there was enough removed to make a hole. It would have to do.

With the first prayer he'd said in years, Aurelian began the tricky work of contorting his body while upside down, so he could go from the ledge he rested on into the space he'd just made.

If anyone else was waiting on the other side of that hole, he would just have to figure that out when he got there.

LYITA FOUND a space in the room that no one else had claimed yet, about halfway towards the center of the room. She looked at the main door to her left, as fewer people straggled in and stood in different places on various spots of the floor's design. An elderly gentleman walked towards Lyita, and coughed. She realized that she must be standing in his spot. She moved and found another one.

The middle-aged woman who'd been staring at her nodded and sneered, as if having had a suspicion confirmed.

The door closed. "And so!" a man's voice called out. Lyita saw a tall, thin and aristocratic man with short mixed-gray hair take a spot in the center of the room, directly beneath the structure in the top of the dome. "Now let us begin-"

The door opened. Lyita tried not to collapse from relief, as Aurelian stepped in. He closed the door behind him. She noticed bleeding knuckles on his fist.

"Any other latecomers?" the aristocratic man in the front of the room asked in annoyance.

"Apologies," said Aurelian. Lyita watched as woman who smirked at her stared at Aurelian. This time she did not smile. Instead her expression descended into purest malevolence. He returned the woman's gaze with sheer defiance.

"Just take a spot so we can move on," the man declared. Aurelian stood next to Lyita. "Now then, while there still is moonlight let us begin. For those I have not met before," he smiled with light amusement at both Aurelian and Lyita, "call me Roths. In brief, you are present at the renewal of an old truce that keeps all of us and the interests we serve from each other's throats. When it has been broken we all have suffered. Therefore, to help perpetuate our beneficial peace, a spell was made. Every one hundred and thirteen months, we shall select an arbiter. When inevitable conflicts of interest arise, or something affects us all, this arbiter shall speak and their word shall be enforced by all the other groups." He indicated himself. "For the past period, I have been honored to serve this role. Whoever the spell selects tonight will take my place, for the next one hundred and thirteen times the full moon shines upon St. Petersburg." He spread his hands. "Are we all ready for the ceremony to begin?"

Most of the group nodded.

"We are not!" the middle-aged woman declared.

"Yes Magda?" asked Roths. "It seems you have something to say."

She snarled and pointed at Aurelian and Lyita. "They were not invited here. They should not be a part of this."

"Nevertheless, they are here. That simple fact proves their right to attend. No one who learns of this can be forbidden, you know that. You also found your way here yourself, years ago. This is the heart of the truce that serves us all."

The woman known as Magda clenched her fists. "Fine then. They shall be dealt with soon enough."

Roths nodded. "All are in, the doors are closed. Let us begin." He spread his arms forward, and his hands began to glow. "The doors to heaven rise." Above him, the light began to shift. The patterned metal lattices in the highest part of the dome separated into two sections, and began to rotate in opposite directions. Slowly at first and then with increasing speed, they spun.

The moonlight came in brighter from above, and was

broken into shifting patterns of light and shadow by grid at the dome's top. A circle of light formed in the air above them, with wisps trailing from the edge. Roths' hands shined with almost painful brightness, and then the light drifted from them in fist-sized spheres to merge into the circle.

Seeming of it's own will, the circle drifted downwards. Aurelian saw that it was headed towards the woman called Magda

"You must be joking," Aurelian blurted out.

Roths frowned. Even the mist seemed to pause and wait, as all of the attendees turned towards Aurelian.

"Why do stare at me like a bunch of goats?" Aurelian protested. "Tell the truth and shame the devil. She had to steal luck just to get in here. That bitch couldn't run a coffee shop."

"That common peasant has no business here," said the woman. "He doesn't even know magic!"

"Yet I got in here in anyway," said Aurelian, brandishing his bloody knuckles. "And I didn't even have to steal anyone's luck. How do you like that?"

She turned to the crowd. "This cheap peasant thug killed my dear friend and servant Oleg! Along with his whore, who has the nerve to stand in Oleg's place. Are we going to let these street rats do this to one of us?"

"Watch us do it again to you," said Lyita. "She tried to run at Magda, and found she could not move her feet. They were bound to their space on the marble floor.

"None of us can move," Roths explained. Not until the nest arbiter has been selected."

The older man in the bus uniform faced Lyita, petting his cat as he raised an eyebrow. "That 'bitch', as you call her, is Magda. Purloined luck is only one of her ventures. She runs one of St. Petersburg's strongest occult concerns."

"So?" Aurelian challenged. "This assistant of hers tried to kill us, and did kill a poor kid just trying to go to college. You want to give her more power? You think you can trust someone like that?"

"This troubles me personally," Roths admitted. "I don't like murder or theft, if it is avoidable. But both are within our law, as long as only the non-magical are harmed."

Magda nodded, satisfied. "Thank you for remembering our law. I expect no less, and as arbiter I will do no less."

"You haven't been selected yet," Roths reminded her.

"Then let us move forward!"

"Now I object," said the man with the cat. "If these two are truly non-magical peasants, then their attendance is traceable to your failures. I do not know if you should be a candidate for arbiter."

Magda snarled and made a dismissive motion with her hand. "Sometimes vermin show up, and need extermination."

To Aurelian's dismay, several in the group nodded their agreement. He jabbed his finger at Magda. "If you're so fancy and great, why'd you need to take my luck then?"

"I don't!" said Magda. "That was all my assistant."

"Then you should be able to defeat this mere peasant," said a rather elegant younger Asian woman to Magda's right. "Having found out who you are, it is within his rights to challenge you."

"You're damn right I do!" said Aurelian. He had no idea where this going, except that it probably wasn't good. The only path that seemed worse at this point was backing down.

"And I challenge you too!" said Lyita.

The Asian smiled lightly and shook her head, as if admonishing a child. "Women peasants cannot challenge. I am sorry."

Lyita's eyes flashed fire. "Free my legs and this peasant will claw your eyes out."

Roths moved his hand and Lyita could not speak. "We don't have much time. The moon moves through its positions, and we must select a new arbiter before the time has passed." He turned to Magda. "This young man has challenged you. Do you accept?"

"Of course I do," she snapped.

"Then let's go forward."

Magda breathed in, and held up her hands. The same patterns appeared that Aurelian had seen in the alley. She looked into his eyes, nodded and smiled with gleeful malice. A glowing yellow mist came grew from her hands, and solidified into a tendril, edged in black. Seconds after it left, it was followed by another. One after the other they snaked their way through the immobile crowd towards him. He watched, unable to move, as he saw they were headed straight for his heart.

The first tendril slithered through the air, aiming for his heart. He tried to knock it away with his hand, and his nerves screamed with pain and then went cold. It was just enough to nudge the band away. It continued past him in the air, and began arcing back. He could no longer move that arm.

She laughed. "This will be over soon." The tendril snaked around the room, to slowly make its way back to him.

"You can't trust her with whatever this role is!" Aurelian implored the group. "When her time comes, she won't surrender something like that once she has it. That's not the kind of person she is!"

"If she is not worthy, you can prevent her," said the man called Roths. "You and your friend you clearly care for each other very much."

Magda smiled with calm certainty as the next tendril edged ever closer. It was joined with the first tendril that had hurt and numbed his arm, now edging back again his way.

Aurelian thought as hard as he could. He had nothing. All he had right now was his life and Lyita, and he was about to lose them both.

Something about what that man Roth had said…

Aurelian looked over at Lyita, and felt how much place she had taken in her heart. If he didn't live, at least she should. It wasn't right that she should suffer his fate too.

In the moonlight, he saw a purple mist start to form between him and Lyita. In some way, it looked like what he felt for her.

It was all he had, and he saw nothing else to work with. Without even understanding what he was doing, he tried to will all his feeling into that mist.

It grew.

He redoubled his efforts, and in his tension almost lost his grip on the emotion. He regained his awareness of the feeling by staring deep into Lyita's brown eyes.

The purple cloud between them grew. He could feel the caring from her as well, as she cast her own heart into whatever they were creating.

"What is this?" Magda snarled. "Who among you is helping them?"

Whatever it was that Aurelian and Lyita were manifesting. it solidified between them into planes. The planes became a wall, and moved until it stood between Magda and themselves.

The first of the two tendrils Magda sent at him hit the purple wall of mist. It faded. Magda closed her eyes and breathed in, her hands becoming fists. The second of the yellow-black bands intensified, and managed to make it through the mist. Grabbing his paralyzed arm in his right one, Aurelian batted the tendril away again. He barely felt the sting this time.

Then fear struck him, and the mist shrunk almost into nothingness. He saw Magda smile, and begin even to laugh. He tore his gaze away from her, and back into Lyita's eyes.

He felt pure kindness coming from Lyita. He knew the goodness inside her and felt it move into the space between them.

The wall resumed its former size, and intensified. Magda ground her teeth, and pointed her left finger straight at Aurelian. Two of the remaining tendrils disappeared, leaving 3 to remain.

The tip of her pointed finger began to grow, as she drew the same pattern the luck thief had on his stomach. Aurelian began to feel that same drain from his gut. The purple wall began to fade.

If he lost much more of whatever she took from him, the wall protecting he and Lyita would disappear and both of them would die.

Desperate for a win, Aurelian tried to send the purple wall protecting them straight towards Magda's head. It faded well short of her, and the drain he felt intensified.

Magda laughed out loud.

Aurelian and Lyita suddenly snapped into a fully synchronized will. They pushed the mist forward as one.

Magda redirected all of her floating tendrils to wrap against the wall and push it back.

Both tendrils and wall were destroyed together.

Aurelian and Lyita both blinked. If they hadn't been frozen to the floor they might have fallen. They had not realized how deeply they had melded together, until they were separated.

Magda stared at the space where the tendrils had been broken. "It is against our law to help either side of a duel! Which of you is helping them?"

"The laws say you can't help someone attack," Roths pointed out. "No laws say you can't help defend."

"No!" Magda bellowed. "I must be the next arbiter. It's what I born to do! Listen you all, we are running out of time!"

"*We* are not running out," corrected Roths. "*You* have run out. You have not defeated your challenger, and he has not defeated you. Therefore the moonlight shall pick again." He closed his eyes, and let his hands open. The moonlight began to pour into the room and pool in the air above them.

For a wild second, Aurelian wondered if the moonlight was going to pick him. But it wandered past, briefly to pause near the elegant Asian woman before settling around the apparent bus driver and his cat.

The moonlight faded. The man who'd been selected nodded at everyone else, and then back towards Roths in the middle of the circle.

The attendees began to move freely. Roths walked over and shook briefly shook the new arbiter's hand, and scratched his cat behind the ears.

With that, the ceremony was apparently complete. The gathered began to disperse, some of them chatting briefly to acquaintances and others leaving with no words at all.

Aurelian and Lyita found they were free as well. He took her hand.

"You're my luck," he said.

As the rest left the chamber Magda walked towards Lyita and Aurelian, her face contorted in fury.

Roths stepped between them. "As I'm sure the new arbiter will remind you, there can be no reprisals on the evening of a selection."

"Your time will come," she said. "All of you." She left without a further word.

Roths man coughed, somewhat embarrassed. "It appears you have earned an enemy. If I were you, I would be in no hurry to leave the chamber." The last of the other attendees left, and the doors closed behind them.

Roths looked down at Aurelian's hand. "I notice you may have dealt with our security a bit roughly.

"Nah, I was lying, I didn't touch him," said Aurelian. "I told him someone outside had a counterfeit ticket, and when he went to check I locked him out. Then my luck left and I hurt my hand on the door."

Roths laughed. "If you survive Magda, you will do well."

Will we survive her? Aurelian wondered to himself. "Thanks for helping us live through tonight. "

"I am glad you listened well enough to take the hint. When people care for each other, they can overcome whatever their luck may be. It may not be a lot, but more often than not it is enough."

"For now at least," said Lyita.

"You two have also shown yourselves to be pretty adaptable in the face of true strangeness. That sort of resourcefulness is not to be overlooked." Roths stroked his chin and gave a chuckle. "How did you cross her path?"

"I was looking for work," said Aurelian. "She and her

scumbag must have known a lot of desperate people would be there, so she could take the last of what little luck they have."

Roths laughed. "So you're looking for work? Isn't that just perfect. You see, I'm looking for someone to employ." He rubbed his face. "This really is some luck. Would you happen to have any experience as a thief?"

ABOUT THE AUTHOR

James Beach is a writer, photographer and recovering musician. He was born and raised in New Jersey, and was once told he was a bad Photoshop superimposition on the East Coast. He successfully escaped and now lives in San Francisco, a perfect locale for exploring his emerging super powers.

For more declassified information, visit
jimbeach.net